Fido

and the Fires

The *Fiddle* series:

Fiddle and the See-Throughs
Fiddle rescues the mother of her first See-Through friend from Napoleonic France. (1805)

Fiddle and the Flint Boy
Fiddle is trapped in the Stone Age flint mines of Cissbury Ring. (4,000 BC)

Fiddle and the Headless Horseman
Fiddle defeats the earl who built the barbican gate of Lewes Castle. (Early 14th century)

Fiddle and the Falling Tower
Fiddle and friends try to stop Thomas Cromwell from ruining Lewes Priory. (1538)

Fiddle and the Smugglers
Fiddle and boys from Piddinghoe save Tom Paine from a murderous gang. (1768)

Fiddle and the Fires
Fiddle helps a boy from Every's Foundry escape from the workhouse to fight the New Poor Law. (1835)

Fiddle
and the Fires

Alison Jolly

With illustrations by Helen Stanton

Text copyright © Alison Jolly, 2013
Illustrations copyright © Helen Stanton
With thanks to historians Colin and Judy Brent, Sarah Hitchings
and Paul Myles; to Robert Oaks for foundry technology; to
Walter Hall for handwriting; and to Arthur M. Jolly, editor.

British Library Cataloguing-in-Publication Data.
A catalogue record for this book is available from the British
Library.

ISBN 978-1-907242-45-8

Published by Jolly Books,
32 Southover High Street, Lewes, Sussex BN7 1HX

Printed by 4Edge, 7A Eldon Way, Hockley, Essex SS5 4AD

A story for Frances and Walter,
Robin and Kai

1

The heat hit her like a wall. Fiddle squinched up her eyes against it. When she opened them, she was in a black cave of a room. Black machinery and ladders. The heat radiated from from a menacing black cylinder: it stood taller than a man. A man wearing primitive goggles took a long pole and knocked away a plug. White-hot liquid poured out of the cylindrical furnace into a tipping basin, a solid stone bucket that hung from a crane. Another man tipped the stone bucket foward.

White-gold glare from the tipping basin lit the faces from below like masked servants of the tall black furnace. They poured the molten iron into a box on the floor, its cover held down with bolts as though the iron might escape like a blazing demon.

Fiddle knew what had happened. She had stepped out of time.

Again.

That afternoon her mother had dragged Fiddle to a exhibition in the old Phoenix Iron Works which was once the industrial heart of Lewes town. Fiddle grizzled and then yelled: "I DON'T WANT TO GO TO SOME STUPID MUSEUM!"

Nonetheless, Fiddle's mother insisted in that tone of voice that doesn't allow for contradiction.

Once there, Fiddle went on being grumpy but she was interested in spite of herself. The factory was a huge space with iron beams and hooks in the ceiling, and hundred-year old photographs of fifty or a hundred workmen together. She went so close to one photograph that when she blinked, she slipped through a thin place into another world.

It wasn't like the photo, though. There were only four men in the small black room. The men's sweat drew pale lines down the grey dust on their faces. Through a small window she could see a dappled grey horse plodding round and round a great wheel linked to a snail-shaped fan that pushed air into the furnace. A boy led the horse. Then, as the men poured the blazing iron into its mold, he came indoors to join the others.

Fiddle almost turned tail. She nearly shut her eyes and stepped backwards to escape into her own world – but then the boy looked at her and winked.

2

Most people can't see See-Throughs: transparent people from other times who inhabit Lewes. When Fiddle went through a thin place into a different time she became a See-Through herself. Then most people of that time couldn't see her, either. This boy obviously could.

Fiddle did her best to wink back. She wasn't very good at it. She kept batting both eyes at once. The boy's mouth opened in an O of surprise. He grinned. Fiddle giggled. The boy had blond hair, a round face, bright blue eyes and a dimple in his chin. His wide mouth seemed made for smiling in spite of all the grime.

"'Ere you, Stevie!" shouted one of the men. "What're you goggling at! Go brew us up tea."

The men tipped the stone basin upright. They mopped their brows with rags, smearing the grey dust rather than cleaning it. The light from the basin dulled to bright orange, then cherry-red, then sinister greyish crimson.

One said, "That went well, boys." The others answered, "Thank'ee Mr Every." "That it did, Mr Every!"

Stevie hurried over to them carrying steaming tea-mugs. They sat down on boxes to drink their tea. The tired horse stood still.

Stevie furtively unrolled a piece of rough paper. Fiddle crept up to see. She loved art herself, and she was really impressed by Stevie's drawing, a neat pattern of circles.

"That's a super picture!" exclaimed Fiddle.

The boy jumped. "I can see right through you – you're a See-Through! I've seen them before. But you can talk! You're the first one that ever talked!" he said.

"I think we are special. Most people don't even see See-Throughs. And they don't believe it when we try to tell them."

"Where did you come from?"

"I came through a thin place in the old Phoenix Iron Works."

"Thin place?"

"Yes, in that wall over there. If I shut my eyes I can go back through . . . Anyway, I really like your picture."

"I wish I dared show it to Mr. Every!"

"You could try!" said Fiddle.

Stevie looked over his shoulder at Fiddle. She moved her hands as if she was pushing him.

"Go on!" she whispered. Stevie went to stand by Mr Every, shuffling his feet, and then said all of a rush, "Sir, please Sir, please may I show you something?"

"Of course, my lad."

Stevie carefully unrolled the piece of paper.

"I made this drawing for a casting – maybe a little cover for something. Is it . . . is it all right?

Mr Every looked at the picture seriously before he answered. Then he asked, "Do you really want to become a foundryman, Stevie, and make things out of iron?"

"Oh yes, sir! Yes! I am so glad to have the job here! It would be wonderful to know how to draw patterns and cast them in iron . . . if only I can."

Mr Every smiled, but he just said, "We shall see, Stevie. We shall see. If you make more designs, show them to me."

3

The outer door of the workshop opened. A shaft of sunlight cut through the little foundry. A tall thin man stood silhouetted in the light from the door. He wore a frock coat and a shiny black top hat which made him even taller. Behind him followed a boy in a short cut jacket and very tight trousers and a shirt with a wide white collar.

Fiddle took one look at the boy and knew she didn't like him. Man and boy had identical snooty expressions, as though they looked down on the whole wide world.

"Mr Every?" asked the man. "Can you direct me to Mr John Every?"

"How do you do. I believe I am addressing Mr Thomas Robertson?"

Mr Every didn't offer to shake hands. The foundry owner's hands were grey with the dust of coked coal. Mr Robertson's hands were sheathed in yellow kid gloves.

"I hardly expected to see the head of a successful business working alongside his labourers."

Mr Every answered in even tones: "I am a master ironworker. We were casting a particularly difficult piece. It is as well to have my expertise on hand."

"Very well, then." Robertson's voice was still disdainful. "I have come to see if you would undertake to make an iron gate for the Southover Church graveyard. A gate that will testify to the generosity of the Robertson family toward the church. Is that within your capacity?"

"By all means. We undertake any ironwork, no matter how large or small. Come into the office where we can discuss designs and terms."

The two men went out through another door, but the boy in the jacket lingered. He looked slowly round at the furnace and the tipping bucket and the crane, the grey horse, the grimy men and the very grimy boy. His lips curled into a sneer. "Do you wash in a coal-scuttle?" he asked.

Stevie's fists clenched. He started to reach forward, as if to wipe his dirty hand down that white collar. The other boy gave a frightened squawk and scooted into the office after his father.

4

Stevie gathered up the tea mugs and took them over to a stone sink. He dipped water out of a barrel into a basin to wash them.

Fiddle said, "I'm glad you showed him your picture!"

"Maybe special people should be friends? Can you come back?"

"I think so. Where can we meet up?"

"I know – my mother said we're going to Southover Church on Sunday. Can you come back Sunday when I'm not working?"

"OK! See you then!"

One of the men called, "Stevie! Finish off there! Them mugs ain't the King's best china. Give us a hand here!"

Fiddle found the thin place where she'd arrived. She shut her eyes and put her hands on the wall, and then stepped stepped boldly forward. She was back in her own world just a few minutes after she'd left.

"Time to go home now!" said her mother. "You seem to have enjoyed the Phoenix Ironworks exhibit after all. I'm so pleased!

"But oh, Fiddle, how did you ever get your hands so dirty! They are all grey and gritty!"

"It was the wall of that horrible dirty foundry."

"It's not a foundry any more. They really should keep this museum much cleaner than they do! Here, take a tissue and wipe off your hands until we can find a place to wash up properly."

Fiddle said, "It IS a real foundry! White hot molten iron and a kind of grey coal! And a nasty man in a big black top hat came in."

Her mother looked at her and said, "Oh my Fiddle, are you starting another of your imaginary adventures? I hope this one isn't scary!"

"I promised to go back."

Her mother smiled that kind of knowing smile that parents use about a made-up game.

5

Fiddle made it to Southover Church just as the congregation came out after the Sunday service.

The proud family emerged first. There was the father and his sneering son. The mother followed. She wore a dress with great big balloon shoulders so wide that she couldn't go through the church door beside the other two.

Fiddle looked for Stevie. At first she didn't know him. He was all cleaned up: face scrubbed, hair trimmed, and a clean jacket – only the jacket was two sizes too small, with his wrists showing at the ends of the sleeves. A tall, thin, blond-haired woman held him by the hand. When the proud family drew beyond the other church-goers, she stepped in front of them and barred their way.

"Let us pass, my good woman!" said the father.

"Sir, it's me, Mary Simmons. Mary that was your housemaid these twelve years gone."

"Mary? Mary? Ah yes. I did not recognize you."

"I have asked for nothing these twelve years. But now I beg of you, sir. Now you must care for my son Stevie."

"Your son! Your son! I have no obligation to your son."

"You do. You know that you do, indeed, sir."

"Nonsense!" said the man.

"I beg of you, sir. It is the last wish of a dying woman."

The wife with the puffed-out sleeves spoke sharply. "She's ill! Perhaps she is mad! Thomas, come away from her quickly!"

Fiddle saw that the woman called Mary was shivering violently, in spite of the sun. Over her sharp cheek-bones two red fever-spots blazed on her pallid skin.

The boy Stevie spoke for the first time. "She has the ague, sir. It's bad. She got up out of her sick-bed to speak to you."

The man said "The new workhouses are set up to deal with people like you!"

His wife said even more sharply, "Thomas! William! Come away!" As she pulled her boy close to her, William piped up: "Father, come away from these dreadful people!"

The family hurried down the street. The woman called Mary drew herself up to her tall height, and shrieked after them, "My son will live, but your son will die in flames!"

"No, Mother, no! Don't curse them!" cried Stevie.

It was too late. The words were said.

6

The woman slumped. She had used the last bit of her strength to confront the proud family. She leaned heavily on Stevie's shoulder. He looked about for a place she could rest. He unlatched the gate to the churchyard. He led his mother to one of the graves built like a stone table, called an altar-grave. She collapsed onto the stone.

Fiddle didn't think she should follow, but Stevie beckoned her desperately, as though he could use any help at all, even from a See-Through little girl.

Mary Simmons stopped shivering and began to sweat instead. Her pale face flushed bright red and her breath came in gasps. She let herself fall back to lie flat on the altar-grave stone.

"Mother, Mother!" moaned Stevie, rubbing her hands with his.

"I should not have cursed them . . ." whispered the woman, "not cursed a child. Stevie, if it is in your power, promise me to lift the curse."

"Mother, don't worry about those people. Just get well! Just get well!"

"It is the end, Stevie. You must be brave. When you find your father . . ."

"My father! You said my father died long ago!"

"He is not dead. Your father . . . Your father . . ."

"Who is my father?"

"Your father is . . ."

But the woman could speak no more. With a rattling sound, she ceased to breathe.

7

Stevie looked up, his face stricken. He did not begin to cry. Not yet.

Fiddle gasped in horror. She had never seen someone die like that – she never thought she would see it. The woman lay still upon the altar-grave.

The sexton appeared, the official in charge of the church-yard, a small, round, busy little man.

"What's all this! What's all this! What's all this!" he exclaimed. "Not allowed! Not allowed at all! No sitting or sleeping on the graves! Most improper! Get up, Ma'am. Get up at once."

Stevie just looked at him without speaking.

"Is that your mother, boy? Wake her up! Wake her up at once! Most improper!"

He peered closer.

"Oh dear. Oh deary me! Not dead! She *is* dead! Most improper! No dying in the graveyard! Call the undertaker at once, boy. She must be seen to, and then buried properly. Inside a grave, not on top of one."

Stevie found his voice at last. He said simply, "We have no money."

"No money! Do you mean she is a pauper? A pauper? She must be put in in the pauper's common grave at the end of the churchyard. A pauper's funeral! See to it at once. And the authorities will see to you. Pauper orphans belong in the workhouse."

Stevie was doing something strange – unbuttoning the collar of his mother's dress. He drew a cord from round her neck. Something shone for a moment in his hand. The Sexton started forward. "No tampering with the dead! Pauper's goods belong to the church that buries them!"

He made a lunge toward Stevie. Fiddle tried to grab the man's arm, forgetting for a moment that here she was only a See-Through. Of course his arm went right through her transparent hand. She desperately kicked a vase full of dead flowers in his way. The sexton stepped right into the vase. He sprawled forward, almost flying, and landed full length on his round little tummy.

Stevie ran, ran, ran out of the churchyard gate. He ran and cried at the same time, but he still ran much faster than the fat little sexton who had pulled himself to his feet and was puffing along behind.

Off the Cockshut lane Stevie suddenly swung right and disappeared into a copse of trees by a farm field with Fiddle close behind. When they were safely hidden deep among bushes, Stevie finally let himself burst into real crying.

Fiddle wasn't sure what to do. She wasn't used to touching people she didn't know, but it seemed right to hug Stevie's shoulders until his tears slowed. She passed him a tissue to blow his nose, and he rubbed his sleeve across his eyes.

"What will you do?" she asked.

"We don't have anything left. We couldn't even pay the rent on our room this week. The landlord said he'd turn us out, even with Mother so sick – but I won't go to the workhouse. I can't help my mother any more. I can't even save her from being buried as a pauper . . . All I can do for her sake is stay alive. She said I would stay alive! The work at Every's Foundry is enough to buy my food. I'll sleep outdoors. And I won't go to the workhouse!"

"Who are that awful family? Why wouldn't they help you?"

"Their name is Robertson. Mum always said that if I was desperate, go to them, but she never would. And then she tried, and then . . . and then they just let her die. She's dead and I hate them! I hate them!"

8

When Fiddle came home she cried and cried. Her mother held her and tried to find out what was wrong.

"She died," sobbed Fiddle. "Stevie's mother died. He was right there and he saw her die. And a man came and said she has to have a pauper's grave. That's something awful, I know."

"Oh how sad!" exclaimed Fiddle's mother. "That poor boy! Is Stevie in your class at school?"

"No . . . no he isn't." Fiddle was much too upset right now to try explaining about See-Throughs. Anyhow, it never did any good.

Her mother asked, "What did she die of?"

"She had the ague."

"The ague? I think you must have that wrong, dear. Ague is an old word for malaria. People haven't had malaria in Lewes for – oh, almost two hundred years. Not since the railrway came, when they drained the marshes round the Ouse River and got rid of the mosquitoes."

"Oh."

"Does Stevie have a family to take care of him?"

"I don't think so, Mummy. I . . . I . . . I think I'll have to go back and find out."

9

Fiddle did go back, but Stevie wasn't at the foundry, or the churchyard, or anywhere. She looked for him for two whole weeks, but he was gone . . . as though he'd vanished into thin air

Fiddle kept asking her mother questions about a time with top hats and wide-shouldered dresses and a king, until her mother said in some annoyance, "Why don't you go look it up in the library? It sounds like the reign of King William IV, just before Queen Victoria. But you ask the librarian, not me! I don't know all the answers!"

The Lewes librarian was amused and impressed that a child wanted to know about the time just before Queen Victoria's reign.

She said, "There was actually a newspaper in Lewes in 1834–35, the *Brighton Patriot and Lewes Free Press*. That should give you lots of information for your school assignment."

Fiddle didn't say that she wasn't doing homework, just looking for a friend. The librarian showed her how to scan the newspaper pages on the computer. The newspaper was really discouraging, though, because it was full of long words written in dense black type.

Then Fiddle suddenly saw a headline of May, 1835:

SCANDAL OF CHILD SLEEPING IN CHURCHYARD

She knitted her brows to read:

𝔅rig𝔥ton 𝔓atriot and LEWES FREE PRESS

SCANDAL OF CHILD SLEEPING IN CHURCHYARD

With the Poor Law now in force, all charitable benefits are stopped unless paupers enter a workhouse. A child was found hidden in bushes in Southover Church graveyard.

The twelve-year-old boy, one Stephen Simmons, fought like a tiger with the church sexton and a watchman until they carried him off bodily to the workhouse of St. Anne's Parish.

But should we wonder that a child preferred to sleep among graves than accept the so-called charity of the workhouse?

"Stevie!" she cried aloud. "They took you to the workhouse!"

"Shh," said the librarian. "Don't disturb other people reading."

10

Fiddle stood in the High Street while horses and carriages and people in top hats walked by without seeing her at all. She thought, "St Anne's Workhouse could be near St Anne's Church. I know where that is."

She walked up the hill toward St Anne's. Across the twitten from the ancient church graveyard she saw a high brick building with high-up windows and a heavy door.

A tall man stood by the door, a man with a bushy black beard and very tanned skin, wearing rough sailor's clothes. He seemed uncertain what to do. He had long thin hands – his hands were trembling. The man clenched his fists. He stepped into the field beside the building, and very slowly circled round it, looking at every entrance: the coal chute, the back and side doors, and so to the front again.

The door opened. A woman appeared with a wicker shopping basket over her arm.

The man stepped forward to speak. He said, "Do you have a boy here named Stephen Simmons . . ."

The woman interrupted him. "I don't know the children's names, and if I did I wouldn't be telling.

Only relatives have the right to ask about them, and the poor mites don't have any relatives who care or else they wouldn't be here. If you want to ask questions, go in and speak to the warden."

Instead, the bearded man turned away down St. Anne's hill.

11

Fiddle thought, "He can't go in, but *I* can!"

She waited until the woman came back. Fiddle crouched half under the shopping basket and slipped inside the front door.

Inside, two separate stairs rose three floors into the air: square narrow staircases turning round like tall towers with a wall between them.

A bell clanged. It echoed through the building. Suddenly the stairs were full of people rushing down from the floors above: women and girls and toddlers on one stair, men and boys on the other. Fiddle cried out in horror. The running children looked like a horde of children's ghosts.

Fiddle hung onto the wall as the ghosts rushed towards her. They were all dressed in grey. They had grey faces and huge hungry eyes. None of them saw her, of course, but she felt the wind of their passing as they ran right through her.

The grey people turned into two separate high bare rooms, with no chance for men and women to meet. They lined up in rows by height – tiny five-year-olds at the front, up to bigger ones and adults.

Some were even paler and thinner than the rest, almost white. The very pale ones kept coughing. Each boy and girl, and then each man and woman, grabbed a bowl and spoon, and held it out to women ladling soup from great cauldrons.

Fiddle had an awful realization. The children were not ghosts. The hunger in their eyes was just plain hunger.

Among them, Stevie stood out like a colour picture pasted onto the greyness, with his bright blue eyes and bright blond hair. He had only been in the workhouse a few days, so he did not look like the rest . . . yet.

12

Fiddle went up to him. "Stevie!" She whispered even though she knew the others couldn't hear her.

His face lit up. Then he put a finger to his lips. As the line inched forward, he took a bowl and spoon and held it out for a ladleful of stew. Fiddle sniffed.

The stew was mostly water, with some peas and a bit of onion floating – no meat and almost no potatoes.

The inmates sat and gobbled it up, every bowl finished in an instant. They gave back the bowls and spoons. Then they filed out. The men and women each went up their own stair, but as they passed in the front hall, Fiddle saw a very old man reach out toward an old women, and she toward him.

"No contact! No contact! Go upstairs at once! It's high time we built a dividing wall across this hall."

The loud angry voice came from a woman in a stiff black dress. She stood in the hall like a policeman to separate the men from the women. The two old people dropped their hands. They each shuffled up their own staircase.

Fiddle climbed the stairs with Stevie and the other boys. The boys' dormitory at the top of the building held narrow beds almost next to each other, with a small wooden box underneath each bed for their few possessions. The boys were so tired they fell asleep almost before they lay down.

"Who was that horrible woman in black?" asked Fiddle.

"That's the warden," whispered Stevie. "Those two old people have been married for thirty years, but men and women aren't allowed even to talk to each other here, let alone touch each other."

Fiddle shuddered. She thought of her own grandparents, who were ever so old but still held hands.

13

"Who are you talking to?" asked the boy in the next bed.

"I'm talking to myself" answered Stevie. "I absolutely have to go to the outhouse."

He went to the stair landing with Fiddle and then out to the sickeningly smelly boys' outhouse shed. They hid behind it to talk.

Stevie whispered, "In the morning we start work again. It's school some days, but if anyone hires us to work, we work instead. It's cheaper hiring poorhouse kids than grown-ups."

"What happened to you after I left?

"Mum's funeral was horrible – they just dumped her in a hole in the ground on top of other corpses. Not even a box. A parson said about ten words, and that's all. I . . . I slept in Southover churchyard just to be near her . . . But anyhow, I kept on working. At the foundry it's really great work!"

"You mean you actually like that terrible place with the fire and all?"

"I'm not scared of fire! Mr Every is ever so clever. He knows all about how to heat iron and mould it into things. He made the crane himself for lifting huge pieces of iron, but it's light enough to be handled by a woman! He never makes us work more than twelve hours a day, with breaks for tea. He says it's too dangerous in a foundry to have sleepy workmen!"

But then Stevie's face fell into a pattern of woe. "But now Mr Every will think I left without telling him, and he won't ever have me back . . . But at least I kept Mother's ring." He dropped his head in his hands.

"Her ring?"

'She never took it off when she was alive. She wore it inside her dress so other people wouldn't see."

'Where is it now? Can you keep it safe?"

"It's in my box upstairs. I rolled it up in my dirty socks to hide it. I'm afraid to wear it for fear the other boys will steal it – or even the warden!"

"Can't you get out of here?"

"They took my clothes away. If I leave in the work-house uniform, they'll catch me and punish me even worse for stealing the uniform. Sometimes they send boys away for seven years to the prison land of Australia, just for stealing enough to eat."

"It's awful . . . awful . . . Are there any grown-ups to help? When I came here, a man seemed to be looking for you. He had a black beard and tanned skin – perhaps a sailor."

"I don't know anyone like that."

"We have to do something. Can you write to Mr Every to have you back?"

"Mum tried to make me learn my letters." said Stevie, "but I'm no good at it."

"I'll find some paper and a pen. I can do the writing. Wait for me! I'll come back!

14

Early next day Fiddle and Stevie struggled to write the letter to Mr Every. When it was done Fiddle tucked it in her pocket, ready to run down to the iron foundry.

The bell rang for the children's breakfast – bowls of gruel: thin oatmeal porridge. As the boys lined up, a mean-faced man divided the line in two. He said, "All children of seven and up will go stone-picking on Juggs Hill today. Line up at the door after your breakfast!"

Fiddle followed to see where they were taking Stevie. The crocodile line of grey children turned down St Anne's twitten to cross over the Winterbourne and then climb up towards Southover High Street. The very pale, coughing ones seemed tired even from that short walk. The mean-faced man switched them on the back of their legs with a birch twig cane to make them go faster uphill.

Stevie was still strong and healthy. He looked around and smiled at being out in the fresh air. But then his face changed. The sneering boy from the church walked by in the opposite direction, on his way to classes at Lewes Grammar School. He spotted Stevie in the line.

"Hey, you're the boy with the mad mother! So you did wind up in the workhouse where you belong!"

"Your family murdered my mother!"

"Mind your tongue, you ragamuffin! My family have nothing to do with you or your mad mother either."

Stevie leaped out of the line and hurled himself on the other boy. The two of them fell down in the gutter. Stevie pummelled his enemy for all he was worth. The other boy kicked and clawed back at Stevie.

The mean-faced overseer sprang forward. His switch fell on Stevie's back, knocking the breath out of him. The other boy's fine school coat was covered with mud and horse manure, and he was clearly going to have a greeny-purple black eye.

"Master Robertson! Master William Robertson!" exclaimed the man. "A thousand apologies! This ruffian boy will be severely whipped. I am so sorry that this should happen to you. Please accept my deepest apologies!"

"My father is a Guardian of your workhouse! You will hear about this!"

"Oh, please do not think badly of workhouse discipline, Master Robertson. This ruffian boy has only just come, and he is clearly bound to end his days in Australia."

"My father will hear about this!" the muddy boy yowled. "My coat is ruined! I can't go to school! I'm going home to tell my father!"

Stevie shouted after the boy, "Tell your father that my mother's curse will fall on him!"

The overseer's switch fell on Stevie's back again, but the man said, "I can't leave all the other children just to whip you now. The punishment you deserve will come tonight."

"Fiddle?" whispered Stevie when the overseer went to the front of the line. "Fiddle, take my letter to Mr Every! I have to get away!"

15

The field on Juggs Hill had a lovely view of the bare, rolling downs. Little fat clouds floated in the blue sky, for all the world like the fat woolly sheep on the hills. But the field was steep and very, very stony. Every spring when farmers till the chalky land, flint cobbles seem to swim to the surface like a school of fish. Every spring, if a farmer wants to plough and plant, someone must clear the stones.

The workhouse children divided into gangs. Each had a portion of the field assigned, with more fields waiting when they finished the first. They worked under the overseer's eye. Any child who sat down or lingered quickly caught the switch. Little ones of seven couldn't lift the heaviest flints. Those were left to stronger boys like Stevie, so they had to work together. They trudged for hours back and forth through the muddy field with their hands cupped around freezing-cold stones.

Stone piles grew into pyramids by the field. One of the pale, coughing boys coughed up blood. He lay down on the wet ground. The overseer didn't bother to make him stand up.

The overseer harshly told the other children to keep on working, Stevie carried a big, lumpy cobble to the field edge. A voice whispered from nearby trees: "Stephen!"

Stevie could see no-one. The voice said again, "Stephen Simmons!" For that moment, the overseer's face was turned away. Stevie slipped into the trees.

A tall man with a bushy black beard stood staring at Stevie. At last he said, "Like your mother. Like your mother."

Then he said, "Do you want to escape from the workhouse?"

"Oh, yes! Yes!"

"Put on these clothes. If you take their uniform they will gaol you as a thief."

Stevie pulled on the shirt and trousers the man held out to him. He shuffled his feet into a pair of worn boots.

"Come with me!" commanded the man.

The two of them ran until they came to a red roan mare hidden among trees. The mare whinnied when she saw her master. The black-bearded man swung Stevie up behind him. They cantered away.

16

> To John Every ESQ,
>
> Please sir this is from Stevie Simmons that worked for you at the foundry. I am in St Anne's workhouse please get me out to work for you
>
> Please sir from Stevie

"What do you think of this, letter, Charlotte?" Mr Every asked his wife.

"He's a good lad!" said Mrs Every. "That boy was so well-spoken and polite and worked so hard, for all his ragged clothes. I swear that before he left us he was sleeping rough, with grass seeds in his hair. But so keen!"

"Why did he disappear, then? And why did he fetch up in the workhouse? If we take him from there, they will farm him out to us as an apprentice. They will keep all his wages. If he's a pauper, how do we know he won't steal, or just disappear?"

"I don't know. But when I looked at him I thought of our own sons."

"He's clearly enterprising. He showed me a drawing of something he thought we could make. It wasn't a bad drawing for a child."

"Shall we try him, then?"

"Very well, Charlotte, if you say so."

"I will go myself."

Mrs Every put on her bonnet. She walked from North Street to the parish workhouse on St Anne's Hill, armed with a note from her husband.

Of course she had no idea that See-Through Fiddle was following behind, desperate to know if the letter worked and whether Mrs Every would really help Stevie.

17

Mrs Every was ushered into the warden's parlour. The warden, the fearsome woman dressed in black, read Mr Every's note through spectacles balanced on her nose. She glared at Mrs Every.

At that moment the door of the warden's parlour burst open. There stood Thomas Robertson, his tall hat in his hands.

"Warden!" he shouted "Warden! Do you know that I am chairman of the Board of Guardians of your workhouse! And do you know that one of your ruffian boys has assaulted my son William!"

The warden sprang to her feet. Her spectacles fell to the end of their cord and bounced on her starched black bosom. She said smoothly, "Welcome, welcome Mr Robertson. You are always welcome at St Anne's Workhouse, which you so kindly govern. Please do take a seat."

"I am not here to sit down! I am here to demand that Stephen Simmons be severely whipped for his misdeeds. His punishment should be a lesson to all the others!"

All three grownups were on their feet, eyeing each other with various degrees of dislike or fury. Fiddle was so scared of them that she hid behind an armchair even though she knew that none of them could see her.

Mrs Every said in a tone of icily sweet politeness, "I am much pleased to meet you, Mr Robertson. I am Mrs. Charlotte Every, wife to master ironworker John Every. I have come here about the same boy. My husband wishes to take him as an apprentice in the foundry."

"You want Stephen Simmons!" the warden exclaimed. "You say you want that ungrateful, disobedient wretch! Thank your lucky stars that you are too late!"

"Too late? Is he ill then? Is he dead?"

"Dead? Of course not. He has run away."

"How can a boy run away from here?"

"He was sent to work picking stones from a farmer's field. The overseer looked away for a moment, and then the boy was gone! I am about to send the porter upstairs to fetch the things from his box so we can burn them."

Thomas Robertson cut in, "He was doubtless fleeing my wrath, after so cruelly mauling my son!"

Mrs Every said, "Surely he can't go far in his workhouse uniform?"

"Now that was the biggest insult of all. He left his uniform by the trees at the edge of the field. He must be stark naked! And the impudent boy left it *neatly folded!*"

Mrs Every's lips twitched. She managed not to laugh at the other woman's outrage, but she murmured under her breath, "Well, my husband did say that boy is enterprising!" And then, aloud, "Good day, Mr Robertson. It seems that your vengeance on Stephen Simmons must wait for another time."

18

Fiddle ran from the Warden's parlour and pelted up the square tower of stairs. A muscular porter was ahead of her, but she dodged past him. She ran to the box under Stevie's bed and flung it open. There was hardly anything in the box: a torn undershirt, a pair of dirty socks with holes in. On the clothes lay a few dead flowers from Southover graveyard.

The porter was just behind her. He recoiled and rubbed his eyes because he saw the box lid fly open apparently all by itself. Then he started forward again as Fiddle grabbed the pair of socks. He swiped at them, but Fiddle was quicker. She ran for the stairs. This time though, no one chased her. The man behind was crossing himself and muttering, "Witchcraft! That boy's box is bewitched!"

Fiddle dashed out of the workhouse and into the graveyard of St Anne's Church. She hid behind a gravestone. She carefully unrolled the socks.

There lay a braided cord of blue silk strands, and on the cord a thin gold ring. A ring with tiny letters and a date inscribed inside.

19

Fiddle searched again for Stevie. The newspaper office was on North Street, not far from Every's Foundry. That day's edition was pasted in the window: it said something about workhouses. It was easier to read with the paper white and the print fresh than it the old, scanned papers in the Lewes Library.

𝔅righton 𝔓atriot and LEWES FREE PRESS

RIOT AGAINST WORKHOUSE

FROM OUR OWN CORRESPONDENT
We attempt to rouse the feelings of our countrymen in whose breasts the milk of human kindness is not quite dried up to use every legal means to repeal this Poor Law!

In Eastbourne, on Saturday last, able-bodied workers were offered 1s 3d in meat and flour, and 1s 3d in money as wages to support them *throughout the week or else go into the workhouse*!

The meeting was for tearing the Relief Officer to pieces, but in the end they put him in a cart and drove him out of the parish. Only one, an infirm old man, was willing to take the relief offered by the workhouse. In the case of a man named Webb, who was accused of rioting before Magistrate Robertson of Lewes, the *defence* made was that Men who were *formerly* paid *sixpence* a day (and many a dog costs his master much more) are now paid *fourpence*.

Members of Parliament must see the necessity of removing this Malthusian Dagger from the bosom of Society!

Fiddle slowly puzzled this out, and murmured aloud, "What's a Mal –Malthusi – Malthusian Dagger?"

A voice behind her said, "It's the Poor Law, Fiddle! That's written by Mr John Justice!"

Fiddle spun around. There was Stevie. But Stevie looked over his shoulder and said, "Come quick! I'd best keep hidden."

The two of them found a narrow alley with a dark place that wasn't overlooked. Fiddle had spent so long hunting for Stevie that she was quite annoyed with him. Now that he suddenly appeared, she stamped her foot and demanded, "So who is Mr John Justice? And why are you hiding? And anyway what's a Malthusian Dagger?"

Stevie said, "I know lots of things now. Mr John Justice told me. A clergyman called Malthus wrote a book to say that poor people just go on having children as long as we have enough to eat. Then the rich people said don't give people parish benefits: it's too expensive, and no use anyway because we'll just have more children and skive off work and scrounge more benefits.

"Last year they passed the New Poor Law. Now farmers can offer people starvation wages. If there's a frost or a lay-off of workmen so a labourer has no money to live, he has to go into a men's workhouse made horrible on purpose. His wife goes into a different part for women. All the children get taken away and sent to another one like St. Anne's. That stops people having children, which Mr Malthus says is the only way to deal with the poor."

Fiddle found it hard to believe any law could be so cruel.

"Who's Mr John Justice, then, that told you this?"

"Remember the man with the black beard you saw before? Well, he saved me from the workhouse. He's called John Justice. He goes to all the meetings of the farm labourers to fight the New Poor Law. He gives wonderful speeches. Then he writes it down in the newspaper. He's a real gentleman, you can tell, for all that he helps poor people . . . Fiddle, there's a meeting tonight. Can you come with me?"

"Well – if you want me to."

Stevie puffed out his chest proudly, and went on, "I get to help Mr Justice! Do come and see!"

20

Stevie said, "I have to buy some food for us. Mr Justice daren't be seen in public."

They walked to the market stalls. Stevie quickly bought four potatoes, one onion and two very thin slices from a flitch of bacon. They looked round to see that no-one was watching, then dashed into an alley. They climbed stairs inside a narrow house. Stevie gave a complicated knock, some kind of code. The tall, black-bearded man opened the door.

"So glad you are back, lad!" he exclaimed. "I don't know how I'd manage without you."

His beard was uncombed, and his dark eyes burned with intensity. Mr John Justice spoke with a deep and surprisingly educated voice for a person living in a small, dank room.

The room was as untidy as any room occupied by just one man and a boy – nothing much in it but an unmade plank bed with a grubby coverlet for the man, and a pallet for the boy on the floor. What was strange, given the poverty of the place, was a pile of newspapers and, beside the bed, a small tower of books.

Mr Justice took the food in his long hands and turned to a pot ready to boil over the few lumps of coal in fireplace. Stevie drew Fiddle out to the landing where they could talk.

"Why is he hiding?"

"Magistrates like Mr Robertson are afraid of Mr John Justice. They're watching to try to catch him in some way, so they can stop him organising the labourers. Then they can send him back to Australia."

"Australia? Was he sent there as a criminal?"

"Shh. Nobody but me knows that. He spent seven years in Australia, but he's no criminal. His brother sent him there on a false charge."

Fiddle thought it was all very peculiar. She wondered about this Mr Justice – if indeed that was his real name.

21

The meeting that night was in a small fuggy room in an inn. Twenty or thirty men crammed inside wearing rough clothes and boots that reeked of sweat and tobacco and an undertone of manure. A couple of women were there too, but they stayed at the back and seemed to be brave even to get that far. Fiddle crouched beside the women, wishing she had never come.

A man in front banged his fist on the table for silence. Then he announced that a speech would be given by Mr John Justice. The tall black-bearded man stood up in front. He stared at each of the men with his dark eyes. He cleared his throat, and spoke.

"My friends! Before the Poor Law Bill was passed, the parish poor had less than *threepence halfpenny* per head to allow them to exist upon. After that law was passed, they have now only *twopence per day* allowed them – or else they go to the poorhouse! Mr Webb here in front was dragged before Magistrate Robertson for rioting because even *fourpence* a day is not a living wage!

"These are small matters to those who enjoy their hundreds or thousands a year, but they are of vast importance to tens of thousands English families!

Any reduction in the poor rates is pinched out of the bellies of poor women and children! I urge you to form a labourers' union to defy this law!"

John Justice's eyes blazed. He waved his hands to emphasise his speech. He went on, punching the air with his thin hands.

"And to administer the workhouses there will be no end of commissioners, assistant commissioners and receivers and payers of the poor. Meanwhile, you starve!"

The men shifted their feet. One called in a hoarse voice, "Fine words, Mr Justice! We can't afford to fight the farmers, whatever they pay us. Or the government! Magistrate Robertson would just lock us up! The workhouse is better than gaol!"

Some of the other men growled their agreement. Fiddle could see that he hadn't convinced the crowd.

"Stevie, she said, "you tell them what a workhouse is really like!"

"You mean – me make a speech too?"

"Go on! You can do it!"

Stevie stood up. He looked very small compared to the heavy labourers with their muscled shoulders and calloused hands. He clambered onto a bench so the crowd could see him. Then he stood straight, and spoke in brave, clear tones.

"I was in a workhouse! We had almost nothing to eat! Us children had to work all day instead of the farmers hiring men like you. The workhouse kept our wages – we never got anything for ourselves. And inside, men and women and children are all separate – if you go into a workhouse, you will never see your family again!"

In the hush that followed, Mr John Justice declared, "The workhouse itself is a gaol – a gaol for innocent people! Now will you join in a labourers' union to fight this Poor Law?"

"We will! We will!" shouted the crowd.

But when they asked for action, there seemed to be little they could do besides write letters to Parliament and to the parish and to the newspapers – letters drafted by Mr Justice.

22

The meeting ended, Three of the men lingered.

"Newspapers ain't going to change nothing." said one of them. "We're taking action now! Are you with us?"

"Mr Webb?" asked John Justice. "Watch out – Magistrate Robertson has already marked you out as a rioter. You dare not get into more trouble."

"I ain't rioting now," said Webb. "I aim to get at the farmers that give us starvation wages because we've got no choice but the workhouse. I aim to get them where it hurts. You're all talk, Mr Justice, but are you with us for real action?"

"What do you mean?"

"Ever noticed how easy it is for a barn to catch fire?"

"No! You can't be planning arson! Incendiary fires! That's a hanging offence – or being sent to Australia for the rest of your life!"

"You're coming with us!" growled Webb. He grabbed Mr Justice's arm, and pulled him along as the group strode from the inn, out onto a path into the countryside.

Stevie had to follow him. Fiddle had to follow Stevie. The children shivered in the night as they stumbled along the farm path.

Mr Justice kept waving his hands as as he argued with the men. Webb demanded, "So you're telling us that we just sit down and starve?"

"There are better ways to change the laws! The government won't care if you burn down barns!"

"Aye, but the farmers will care! And you stay along of us now. because we don't want you trying to stop us!"

They came to a dark building looming up beside a field. The men unlatched the barn door and slipped inside. Webb struck flint and steel. He lit a paraffin-soaked torch, and each of his cronies did the same. The torches' gleam showed stacks of hay in the loft, and bags of potatoes piled high and pigs grunting in their pens.

"Stop! Stop this lunacy!" yelled Mr Justice. "You will be caught and hanged!"

"You are one of us now! You are here with us, and if the magistrates ask who started the fire, it's you – you with all your fine speeches! Get an eyefull of all the loot the farmer has stored here – all them bags of corn, all them potatoes dug up by us, all them riches off the sweat of our backs.

"Mates, do we let the farmer keep it?"

"Go to it, Webb!" cheered the others.

John Justice lunged forward and tried to grab Webb's torch away. Stevie and Fiddle ran to help Justice. Webb fended them off with a kick and hurled his torch into the hay. His mates threw theirs into dark corners where piles of hessian grain sacks made an explosive dust.

As the flames rose the men ran out into the night. Justice and Stevie and Fiddle ran as fast as they could away from the others. They ran to where Justice had left his red horse, mounted her and dashed back into town.

Stevie walked Fiddle quickly to the foundry with its thin place in the wall. Just before they parted, Fiddle said, "Stevie, I have something to give you . . . only I took it to my world to be safe. I'll bring it back next time we meet up."

Then Fiddle was ever so glad to put her hands on the foundry wall, blink her eyes and go through to home.

23

The two children met again by the newspaper office. This time, Stevie didn't even stop to say they must hide. He put down a penny for the paper and whisked Fiddle away into the alley. He shoved the newspaper into Fiddle's hand.

"Is there anything about fires? Burning barns? Read it to me!" he gasped. Fiddle read:

𝔅rig𝔥ton ℘atriot and LEWES FREE PRESS

BARNES BURNED! INCENDIARIES ARRESTED!

On Saturday night the horizon was illuminated by another incendiary fire. The incendiary sallies forth with his lighted torch under cover of night to do his awful work of devastation and ruin. The law has lost its terrors.

"What is wrong?" we ask. What has caused the excited state of the rural population?! Is it the New Poor Law, converted into an engine of tyranny and oppression? There is something rotten in the State!

Whether or not connected with the New Poor Law, two incendiary fires burst out last week. At Chinton, the property of the Earl of Chichester, little injury was done. However at Sutton, near Seaford, the fire consumed two barns with a stack of wheat in each, several hundred bushels of potatoes, and two pigs burned alive.

One individual is in custody for the fire at Chinton, and two for that at Sutton.

Fiddle looked enquiringly at Stevie. His normally rosy face was pale. At last he said, "You saw it. You saw Mr Justice try to stop them from setting fires. But now he'll be hanged. "

"What do you mean?"

The men who really did it will go and accuse him! The paper says that the Watch have caught them. Webb and the other incendiaries will say he told them to burn the barns. That way they can save their own necks – and . . . and Mr John Justice will hang! Magistrates like Mr Robertson have no mercy, and neither does the Lewes Assizes!"

As they emerged, there was a familiar face nearby – the sneering magistrate's son William Robertson, still with a greenish eye from the pummelling Stevie gave him on the way to picking stones on Juggs Hill. Robertson glanced at Stevie. His face changed, but then he looked away.

"That horrible rat is still afraid of me," muttered Stevie.

The other boy started off uphill as Stevie turned down.

"I think it's safe," said Stevie. But Fiddle had caught William's sly expression.

She exclaimed, "I don't trust that boy!"

24

"Thomas! Thomas, I am so worried about William!"

Mrs Robertson snatched at her husband's coat sleeve when he returned from his magistrate's office.

"It's night already, and he is still not back from school!"

"Begging your pardon, sir," said one of the family's gardeners. "Master William said I was to give you this letter when you came back home."

Robertson tore open the note, which was written on a schoolbook page in his son's neat grammar-school handwriting.

> *Dearest Father:*
> *I have seen the workhouse boy Stevie who accompanies the wanted incendiary John Justice. They are hiding in Every's Foundry. If I do not return by dark, please come there with a member of the Watch.*
> *Your obedient son,*
> *William.*

Mr Robertson flung his coat back on, and rushed out of the door, leaving his wife aghast. As he ran through the town he kept saying, "Oh William! Oh, my son! If only he knew . . ."

But when he approached Every's Foundry, the whole sky was alight with fire.

The words of Mary Simmons' curse rang in his ears: "My son will live, but your son will die in flames!"

25

Fiddle had gone with Stevie straight from the newspaper office down to the foundry. Stevie stepped aside to the adjoining stable. Dobbin, the old dapple-grey horse who turned the furnace fan-wheel, lived there. In a second, back part of the stable stood the red roan mare – but no one could see her behind Dobbin.

"Hello, lass!," said Stevie, slapping the mare on the rump. Then he called up toward the hayloft, "It's me, Mr Justice!"

A deep voice answered from the hayloft.

"That's just as well. But it's well we left our room. We should move on from this stable before midnight."

"But look – look at this!" Stevie handed up the newspaper into the darkness above. "The police have caught the men who burned the barns! You're in terrible danger! They are sure to accuse you!"

"My boy, I should never have dragged you into my own crusade against the Poor Law. Now you are tarred with the same brush! No-one will believe my word against anyone else's – not the word of a convict back from Australia."

Fiddle saw something move at the back of the stable. She dashed past Stevie and the horses to see what it was. Crouched behind a loose bale of straw was William Robertson.

"Stevie! Stevie!" she called. "That Robertson boy is hiding here!"

Stevie ran toward the back of the stable, his fists swinging.

Robertson gave a gasp and a jerky movement. He flung out an arm to cover his head – and knocked over a burning oil lamp.

It fell onto the straw. The straw flared up. The mare set her feet, backing as far as her halter would let her, eyes rolling. William tried to kick at the bale to stamp on the fire, a fatal move. The bale separated, with straw alight everywhere and flames licking up towards the hayloft.

"Get the horses out!" shouted the voice from above. "Blindfold their eyes! Horses won't move if they see fire."

The man with the black beard jumped down from the burning loft. Stevie grabbed two old grain sacks, and ran to soak them in the water barrel. He tied them quickly round the two horses' eyes.

The tall man hadn't seen what started the fire. As he started toward the blazing straw bale, William

recoiled, and then dashed up the ladder to the hayloft. He was apparently even more afraid of black-bearded John Justice than of the fire – but the fire caught ever more widely in the tinder-dry stable.

"William is back there! He'll be killed!" cried Stevie. "We have to save him!"

Man and boy plunged toward the back of the stable. Stevie had just enough time to call out, "Fiddle! You take the horses!"

Fiddle had no real idea what to do. She had never even ridden a horse in her own world, but somehow animals always trusted her. She took hold of the halter of each blindfolded horse, and spoke to it calmly. The mare seemed almost turned to iron herself, ready to plant her feet and stay solid until she was burned alive, but slowly she yielded to the little girl's soft voice. Trusting grey Dobbin was more willing to come.

Fiddle led them out into the stable yard. Then she looked back into the inferno of the burning building. The ladder to the hayloft was on fire. The man tried to put his foot on a burning rung. The whole ladder collapsed around him.

"Lift me up! I'll get him out!" cried Stevie.

The bearded man shuddered and hesitated.

"Quick! Don't wait! I'll get him out!" cried Stevie again.

The bearded man lifted Stevie high in his arms and threw the boy up into the blazing hayloft. Stevie disappeared into the fire.

Then Stevie was back at the edge of the loft. He dragged a limp form behind him. He shoved it over the edge, down into the man's arms. He jumped down himself with the ends of his hair blazing. The man caught him, quickly rubbed out the fire in his hair, and carried both boys out into the open.

"He's badly burned!" exclaimed the man. "He needs cold water to cool the pain. Help me put him into the water barrel."

The two of them lifted the fainting form and plunged him into the barrel, while Stevie splashed water over his own head.

Then Stevie stood with his arms around William Robertson, holding the other boy's head safe above the water. Stevie had saved William's life from the flames and lifted his mother's curse.

26

The town's two fire engines pumped in double time, two men pushing up and down on either end of the handles like a frantic see-saw. A brigade of water carts rumbled over the cobbles, feeding the pumps with water from the Ouse river. Twenty or thirty men carried buckets to help the firemen, while round the edge stood hordes of spectators watching the fire. The street was alive with fire – licking from the stable onto the wooden fabric of the foundry itself.

Thomas Robertson pushed madly through the crowd. "My son is in there!" he cried. Another man grabbed his arm. "Come round with me. I can find a way in, if anyone can. We must try it from the river side." Robertson in his anguish barely recognized that the other man was Mr Every.

The two men ran, slipping in the riverside mud, until Every produced a key that unlocked the back door of the stable yard. They rushed in to a scene of black figures silhouetted against the flames of the burning buildings behind. There stood a man as tall as Robertson, with a bushy black beard. There was a boy with scarecrow hair, blond ending in black burned tips, holding up the shoulders of another boy inside a water barrel.

Two horses stood calmly in spite of the fire beyond, just as though someone they trusted was caring for them.

"William! Oh my William!" cried Mr Robertson. "What have they done to you!"

William spoke clearly, though weakly. "Father, it was all my fault. In the fire I prayed that if I didn't die I would try to be good and always tell the truth. I started the fire. I knocked the lamp over by mistake but it's still my fault. Then Stevie and this man saved me."

Robertson swung round to the bearded man. He recoiled a pace.

"Stephen!" he cried.

The bearded man answered "Yes, Thomas. Your brother Stephen. You thought you could get rid of me! You thought my radical ideas brought shame on our family – and you plotted to seize my share of our inheritance. In spite of you I prospered in Australia. I read, and I learned – from Thomas Paine and other thinkers – how to campaign for the rights of men. Then I came back to claim my son."

Stevie looked up.

"Are you my father?"

The man gave him a great bear hug.

"I didn't dare tell you for fear you wouldn't want to be the son of a convict – or, now, an outlaw. But the hardest thing I have ever done in my life was to throw you up into that burning loft."

"I'm so glad! I was so afraid my father was Mr Robertson . . .Thomas Robertson!"

The man laughed loud.

"Well, your father is a Mr Robertson – Stephen Robertson. Your mother and I were lawfully married, so your own real name is also Stephen Robertson."

27

Thomas Robertson glared at his brother. "You say this illegitimate boy is your son? You say that he can claim your inheritance! You have no proof!"

Fiddle ran forward "Stevie!" she cried. "I saved this for you!" Everyone had been too busy to notice a little packet of blue silk from their own world floating at the height of Fiddle's pocket. Now she slipped the silken cord with the ring over his head.

Stevie whispered, "Oh thank you! Oh, thank you, Fiddle!' He stepped forward with the same brave voice he had used to make his speech to the labourers. He held the ring out toward his father and uncle.

"Here is the proof!" he declared. "Her ring! My mother's wedding ring with your own initials, father: S.R. and M.S. and the date of your marriage, May 9, 1823."

Thomas Roberston exclaimed, "You actually married the housemaid!"

Stephen Robertson shouted at his brother, "My wife Mary Simmons was the finest person I have ever known! It was she who taught me that honesty and courage and quick wits have nothing to do with wealth or fine breeding! And Mary has raised our son to be as honest and strong as herself!"

Thomas Robertson seemed about to snarl an answer, when William's voice cut into the quarrel between the two tall men. His voice cracked with the pain of his burns, but it held a soft tone that somehow stilled the angry shouting.

"Father! Father! I prayed to be a good boy and good man. Stevie is my cousin: he has his mother's ring. When I am grown, I will share my inheritance with him. Stevie and his father saved my life from the flames!"

Thomas Robertson seemed to crumple, to become shorter and smaller and thinner and much, much older. After a long while he muttered, "I have been rebuked . . .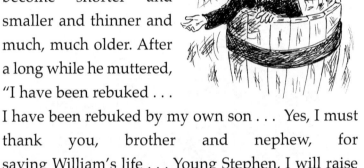

I have been rebuked by my own son . . . Yes, I must thank you, brother and nephew, for saving William's life . . . Young Stephen, I will raise you to be a credit to our family. I will send you to Lewes Grammar School. You can have the education of a gentleman instead of following an outlaw."

Stevie's father said. "Tonight I ride to Portsmouth and take passage to America. In England I face the gallows. I shall go instead to a country where a man may make himself anything he pleases. Come with me, Stevie! we may die on the way or we may find a future of adventures in a new land!"

Stevie looked from his uncle to his father, and then faced Mr Every. There was a pause. Finally Mr Every said, "Stevie, I cannot make you a gentleman or give you adventures. If you stay with me you can only become a foundryman. But this whole town is about to change. The railway will come to Brighton and Lewes. There will be iron rails and iron rail stations and all along the sea-front new railings made of iron, and grand new iron piers built into the sea. My foundry will rise like a phoenix from the ashes of this fire: I shall call it the Phoenix Iron Works. If you stay here you can be part of the greatest change that Sussex has ever known. That is what I offer you."

Stevie turned slowly to each of the three. At last he said, "Uncle, I'm no gentleman. What I ask of you is a stone to remember my mother. She lies in a pauper's grave. Give her a real gravestone in Southover churchyard in her true name of Mary Robertson."

"And Father, I love you. I love that you came home to find me. But my life is not like yours. I will take your name and my mother's – and I'll learn to read so that I can read your letters from America.

"Mr Every, I've always wanted to be a foundryman. Perhaps I can help make patterns for the new railway station in Lewes! If you will take me back, I would like to join the Phoenix Iron Works."

28

Charlotte Every had run from her house to the fire and into the stable yard just in time to hear Stevie's choice. She nodded to her husband and put her motherly arms around the boy.

She said, "Stevie, you have suffered enough. Now come home with me to sleep in our house with our own sons."

He let his head fall onto her shoulder and shut his eyes. After being so strong for so long, he suddenly looked much younger: a tired child who at last had found the comfort he so badly needed.

Fiddle handed the red mare's halter to Stephen Robertson to ride toward his ship for America. Mr Every took grey Dobbin's and hitched him to a foundry cart to carry William home. Nobody noticed that invisible hands held out the horses' halters. Both horses nuzzled Fiddle before they left – they knew she was there even if the others couldn't see her.

Then she stepped through the thin place, now a gap in the wall with charred timbers around it. She was back in her own world in daylight only a few minutes after she had left.

Tired as she was, she still went home by way of Southover church. Almost all the gravestone names

were too rubbed out to read so she just imagined the
very finest one as Mary Robertson's. Inside the church,
though, hung a memorial to William Robertson. He
had kept his fire-born promise to become a good boy
and a good man. He lived on for many decades as the
rector of Southover church.

There was no sign of Stevie in the church, but as Fiddle walked toward home on Priory Street she glanced downward and gave a shout of surprise. She leaned over and traced Stevie's design of circles with her fingers on an iron cover set into the pavement.

And then she looked up. She saw the proud pillars of Lewes railway station and the ironwork tracery of its roof.

Fiddle knew Stevie had found his dream at last – and Mr Every's, too – their designs and dreams cast in enduring iron.

THE END

How much of this story is true?

The Robertsons

Three real people with the same last name lived in Southover. Stephen was sentenced at Lewes Assizes to seven years in Australia,1827–1834. Thomas was a Lewes magistrate from 1830–38. William, born in 1827, became rector of Southover. I have changed their last name and made up their characters. Their real name is on William's memorial in Southover church. (Apologies to any surviving family.)

The New Poor Law

Passed in 1834, this replaced laws dating from Elizabethan times. The Elizabethan poor laws treated the very poor as victims of bad luck who needed help from the parish. However, they had to return to their own parish for help, even if they died on the way. Under the law of 1834 the poor were considered as simply lazy or immoral or irresponsible in having too many children. Separate workhouses for men, women, and children were made so unpleasant that only the truly desperate would accept such 'relief'. The New Poor Law's effects were all too real.

The Phoenix Iron Works

John Every started a small iron foundry in North Street, Lewes in 1832, with a horse-powered fan for the furnace and a crane designed by himself so cleverly that even a woman could use it. A fire in 1835 set the date of this story. The Phoenix Iron Works under his son and grandson cast the ironwork for Lewes railway station and shipped huge castings as far as Australia and America.

Its history and stories told by people who worked there are on *www.lewesphoenix.org*

Phoenix Ironworks 1910, by kind permission of the Sussex Archaeological Society

The Brighton Patriot and Lewes Free Press

This was a radical newspaper published by solicitor George Faithfull. The articles on the Poor Law, the labourers' protests, John Justice's speech and the barn fires are condensed from its May and June 1835 issues. The newspaper also championed bringing railways to Brighton and Lewes. The fire-fighting in this story is from a fire in a livery stable on Albion Street in Eastbourne told in the issue of May 5th, started by a workman so tired from 18-hour working days that he did not quite blow out his candle before falling asleep. Four horses died because they panicked and refused to move, as well as a dog who went back into the building to save three of her puppies and was killed by a falling beam when she returned to fetch the fourth.

http://www.bl.uk/reshelp/findhelprestype/news/newspdigproj/ ndplist/

Sussex Past is the Sussex Archaeological Society, a registered charity whose aims are for people to enjoy, learn about and have access to Sussex heritage. The Library in Barbican House holds many historical records including those of the Phoenix Iron Works. The six historic sites of the Society are open to visitors old and young. For more information visit *www.sussexpast.co.uk*

SUSSEX
PAST